Redshift

5

(2020 edition)

ARROYO SECO PRESS

Arroyo Seco Press

Redshift Anthology #5

Edited by Aruni Wijesinghe

www.arroyosecopress.org
www.redshiftmag.org

logo by Morgan G. Robles
morganrobles.carbonmade.com

Cover image: iStock batuhan toker

ISBN-13: 978-1-7326911-4-8
ISBN-10: 1-7326911-4-2

for Michelle

Poems

Redshift

the infinite
inner universe
naked to the eye

Third Things

In order for time to begin, at least
one thing had to end.

The existence of numbers has not
been proved.

The best color is blue, the flame kind.

It's wrong to steal from people
who've forgotten what they have.

Kneeling in prayer is like standing
to look at the moon.

It's a very good idea to steal
from people you wish existed.

Many great writers are just awful.

The worst color is blue, the tooth kind.

If you were better than you are
you'd have no way of knowing.

All gunfire is a mating call.

Donny Jackson

vanessaguillen

the sand in a distant country where blood is planted but doesn't
    grow anything
says to her
you would've been safer here we
say that as
the grit
who dream of being a mirror one day

know that the color of the uniform wouldn't have mattered
    because
all flags understand that even though they can teach a woman
    how to do it killing
is what men do to speak God that is
taking life is a foreign accent for not being able to give life
therefore being a woman about war next to a man is too much
    whole God for some men so
men try to steal God from women about war by forcing
    themselves inside a temple

your death is a runaway captive

sing north star

crosshair them

hymn center mass

belt pinkmist

                every salute is an erection

Iniko

Mornings in Baltimore, Katherine would trundle over to her laptop as the teapot heated up. It was still night in Alaska, so the live cams showed only a mauve haze.

Discovering the Brooks River cameras was the one small, bright spot in the pandemic. A church friend had recommended them in April. In the months since, Katherine had checked in on the bears each day. It was nice to spend time with creatures for whom the word COVID meant nothing. At night, she would leave her laptop running on the bedside table. When she woke at all hours, still alarmed by the absence beside her in the bed, she'd listen to the rushing river and try to relax. She imagined the bears sleeping on the river banks in furry piles, like puppies.

She hadn't hugged or even touched another person since March. Harry was a large man, but still, the heft of the tote bag containing his ashes had surprised her. She'd put it in her closet when she returned from the funeral home. Someday, her niece would mix their ashes together and plant a crepe myrtle by her house.

There were several different live bear cams, depending on your mood. You could watch huge males compete for leaping salmon at Brooks Falls. In a quieter part of the river, you might find a caramel-colored female lounging in the river as if in a bathtub. She'd be eating a salmon while her cubs played nearby. The bears inhabited the river and its banks like confident, relaxed aristocrats.

Sometimes a banner would appear above the live cam footage. "Lions at the watering hole at Tembe!" "Majestic giraffes!" Click the banner, and you could zip to a different locale in seconds. That's how Katherine came to know Iniko. She'd seen an announcement—something about Iniko getting cleaned. Who was Iniko? Iniko, it turned out, was a fluffy gray condor chick who lived in a nest near Big Sur. *Iniko* was a name suggested by viewers. It came from Nigeria and meant "born during troubled times."

In August, a massive wildfire closed in on Iniko's nest, which sat high in a redwood tree. The signal to the camera went down. For days, no one knew if Iniko had survived. Katherine went off her food, felt woozy. Even the rushing river didn't soothe her at night. She wondered if Iniko was now just ashes too. What would a condor chick's ashes even weigh?

Eventually, Iniko was confirmed to be alive and in the nest. Katherine could finally breathe again, but she returned to the bears full-time. She was too old for new heartbreak.

Once, on the underwater cam, Katherine watched two bears who seemed to be dancing together in the water. Their thick, hairy legs clomped and lifted in the turquoise water. They were life itself, buoyant and joyful. Harry would have loved that.

George Hammons

The Cherry on Top

Someone cursed me
No, literally and
I deserved it, I did something
So they unleashed the year that is 2020
It is as if they foretold every morbid aspect, they
Enunciated a shackle that has settled around me
And the cherry on top (of which they did not tell)
Is RBG
She was so ill and yet I am thunderstruck
The whole jolt and spin of it
The screech and crumpling sound of it
The deafness now
And I am not alone (I wonder)
Am I yours or are you my
Collateral damage
Somehow I think kindness and humility are the answers
But I want to throw something, scream!
Stomp!
Hulk Smash!
Or even better VOTE!

Burt Shultz

Erase the name
let the bridge be John Lewis
from now on

Reasons I Don't Sleep at Night

1.
Cancer is not contagious. Neither are car accidents, unless you mean you can catch one by existing in a place a car wants to be. By that logic, bullets are contagious so shouldn't we do something about those?

Oh, right.

2.
To anyone who wants to wrap a flag around their shoulders like a shroud: this is not about you. It's not about Aunt Joanie, or Uncle Chachi either. More than likely, you'll have the stupid luck to get through this untouched. Even if Ralph or Potsie or even Al Delvecchio dies gasping and alone, you'll find a way to blame it on something else. Thoughts and prayers and all that.

No, this is about the Fonz. You know why? Fonzie is the one who has to clean up the family's mess. Whether it's Richie joining a gang, Joanie smoking, or donning a pair of waterskis to jump over a shark because—well, because sharks exist and must be jumped over by men wearing leather jackets and board shorts—he's the Cunninghams' eternal emergency response system.

Except Arthur Fonzarelli didn't have to wear a facemask to hug Mrs. C goodnight, or put on gloves when he bumped the jukebox to life at Arnold's. He didn't have to worry about rate of infection, or comorbidity, or telling kids not to drink disinfectant.

3.
Snake oil.

4.
Look, this disease has nothing to do with Schrodinger. We know what's in the box. Chances are the cute widdle kitty wants nothing more than to go home with you, curl up on your lap in all its absolutely-existing purritude, and make baby kittens. Which will inexplicably visit your neighbors, or go see the home of the clerk at the grocery store, or the houses of everyone who works at the meat packing plant, and make more baby kittens.

Which is fine. Kittens are fine. Of course, there's a slight chance the cute widdle kittens will crawl into your lungs one night, and never come out again. Or you might get a call about how granny's new kitty (which she didn't even know she had adopted) choked her to death last night.

I know, this is a terrible metaphor. If you're really hung up on my choice of symbology for something that could literally kill tens or hundreds of thousands of people then you're missing the point, and you probably should have given up around the time I mentioned the Fonz.

5.

I'm nostalgic for the good ole days when the lies didn't matter. Back when we could laugh about the size of a crowd, or Sharpie Photoshopping. Remember when the Secret Service actually rented trucks to hide how much golf went into a "working weekend at the Southern White House?"

Back when fifteen was almost zero. When 'yuge' was almost funny, and not a way to describe the numbers of the dead. Back when unsolicited medical advice from America's leading bone spur specialist couldn't reach much farther than the other end of a phone?

Funny story: I used to watch the press briefings as a way to forget about what was really going on. Back in the days they were inventing new ways to describe kids in cages. When disasters were disasters, not reality shows. Before this Novocaine presidency settled in.

What I wouldn't give for a reason to laugh.

Juan Delgado

Trying to Fit Them Snugly

A rainbow of bandanas occupies our clotheslines,
the flags of our neighborhoods for now.

In a supermarket of get what you can,
we wear the eyes of half-covered faces,
marking the space ahead.

For our allies, we strap on a field of foxtails
while their words burn, embers at our feet,
caught in a severe storm.

We bounce through the streets en masse,
knowing who muffles our daily pressure,
and who tosses us a slice of bread over our head.

We can't push off the edge of our cities far enough.

Behind the moist breathing,
an eye twitching, a fear of another's
breath widening beyond the tree line,
we fidget, aware there's no leveling
beyond the masks.

John Brantingham

Lizzy

Mid-March I climb into bed early and stream *Cheers* because it demands nothing of me intellectually and because there's no reason not to. Annie's next to me and asks how long it will be until I see my students again.

"I'm not sure," I say. "I think we're going to have to meet on Zoom for a while, but maybe until May or June."

Lizzy, who is part shepherd and part Basenji, is an odd mix between a big and small dog. She's seventy pounds but can curl herself into a tiny ball. This evening, she senses something and chooses to be a little dog. She crawls for the first time to the head of the bed and rests her body against me and lies her head on my chest.

I didn't think I was going to be able to sleep, but the next thing I know it's the middle of the night and Lizzy's still there and maybe ten episodes have gone by.

By April, Lizzy's worked into her new routine, and she waits impatiently until I lie down and start streaming. Part of the ritual now is that I bring snacks for the three of us, and I tell Lizzy that she's a good dog as she settles in. Annie asks me, "Do you know if it was COVID?"

"No," I say, "and I couldn't really ask. I've known him for maybe ten years, but he was a student. I liked him without really knowing his family or friends." Lizzy eats fried vegetable chips off my shirt. She groans as though she doesn't like *Monk*, which is what we're onto now. When I stop petting her head, she looks up at me as if to ask why, so I don't stop.

John Brantingham

Summer comes and with it, it seems that everyone in my town has bought enough fireworks to last from June through August. Explosions light up every moment of sky, and the first night I worry that Lizzy will be frightened. If she is, she's more worried about me than herself because she curls into me as we watch *Psych*.

September brings me a new group of students, and Annie asks me how they reacted when I told them we'd be in online classes through the fall and the spring. "They didn't really react," I say. I think of their faces which stared back at the news impassively. I wonder if that was my expression when someone told me, too. Lizzy licks my face and groans. I rub her head and place a piece of cheese on my chest.

I think about my campus. I think about the mountains. I think about London. I think about Long Beach, and soon I am asleep in the island world of my bed. Annie lies next to me. Lizzy lies ear down on my chest as if she is monitoring my heart.

Alexandra Umlas

Canasta

I kept pages of scores from playing Canasta
on our Honeymoon, hula girls drawn

in the margins, the waved line of paper
where a Pina Colada probably splashed

from its whip-creamed glass. Recently
we've taken to playing again—shuffling

the two decks together, placing same
with same, slipping the wilds at the end,

cards fanned over the swish
of the dishwasher, a bowl of just-picked

grapefruits like small, orange worlds
adjacent on the table. And we don't

play nice. I discard cards I need,
feed you false information,

and you do the same. We are well-paired,
the kids tucked upstairs, anyone's game—

A. León

Quarantine Song

I crack a window
to overhear the dew
evaporating on every weed
in our front lawn, the hiss
of light drying the morning.

I set open magazines
in front of electric fans, imagine
the riffling of pages is wind
through the feathers of Canadian geese
winging across a sky
empty of planes.

I curl myself around the sleeping
cat at the foot of the bed, interpret
his snoring as an oracle that foretells
gentler days, open doors.

I press my ear
to the refrigerator
each time the automatic ice maker
drops more cubes into the bin,
thrill to the contained avalanche
dispensed into my blue plastic tumbler.

I loosen the washers
on each faucet, set the dripping
to different tempos. I need
drops falling into ceramic basins
to measure the passing of days.

A. León

I pour silverfish
onto unevenly stacked books
and listen to them eat
words.

Someone should consume
all this poetry.

Dare Williams

At the March

The way I forget someone's name
gives pain to another

America,
your portrait rests on the tip of my tongue.

I am lost and looking for you,
all this screaming where to put it.

I turn a soft corner, a cold shoulder
to the ones I love.

A crowd is a sea of stones
each wave scrapes my skin.

I see a former lover and then I
see you and then a face

buried deep among strangers
tell me,

Is a person a safe place?
Is a protest a promise?

Cynthia Alessandra Briano

Inscribed: Quarantine Day 40

I am careening, though slowly. In the dream, I am jettisoned into space, loosed from a larger ship. I have to fly a spacecraft that is only a wide strip around me, no wider than the length of my hand, encircling me like Vitruvian Man, except the circle is elastic and tight like a thick rubber band. The perimeter closes in. There are no keys or buttons on the band and nowhere to anchor myself. The only way of orienting it in any direction, I realize, is with my body—shifting the push or contracting against it with my arms and legs. The only way of achieving direction is by balancing the weight and counterweight of my own struggle. I am my own cantilever.

    —viga voladiza sobresale. liga voladiza.

    My body has to start and stop itself in space, with nothing to push off of.

    I already know this task.

I learned it when I was fourteen in boarding school. I joined the diving team, and I had to learn to begin my body's rotation and stop it while I was already careening forward. When we are grounded, pivoting our own body and direction is simply a matter of footwork—we push off or away from the floor. But in the air, the torque has to come from your center, from your core. The movement, if you achieve it, has to start from the outside in, from your hands, arms, and shoulders moving once in the same direction like the blades of a propeller.

It is a decision more than a movement.

Your core is what sustains this decision once you make it. The decision to turn your body in a different direction when you're not grounded seems, at first, futile—every time. There is no force in your arms alone. It is the decision to move that begins the torque itself.

> You only learn this, repeatedly, as you attempt it.
> Each time is full of uncertainty, full of disbelief.

I thought I knew how to move my body through the air from when I did gymnastics as a girl. But even that—the floor is your springboard. Your body flies only after push-off. You are always anchored; you simply learn to spring. It doesn't *look* possible, then you learn to look past. But this was a different way of disbelieving our senses.

Being a diver means you are skeptic of space, a skeptic of your own body's capacity to decide for itself against the laws of forward-going motion that propel us out of control or else against the circumstances that relegate us immobile, static, without wind or grounding, stranded. It is a skepticism that is grounded in the physicality of our senses. Yet to be a diver means to walk yourself out of your own disbelief—only by leaping into it—not with unwavering faith or persuasive action, but with the minutia of movement.

> When you are weightless, the smallest motion propels you forward.

The movement of your hands sets you going—it is the lifting of your arms that makes you stop, face the direction you mean to face. You learn to move through space when there is no anchor. The anchor is you.

The anchor is your decision to take control of your falling.

("To career elegantly," D. said, of the third rail—
how it doesn't keep a train from going off the tracks, only allows it to career elegantly.)

To turn a fall into a dive, or a safer landing—*aterrizar* to come into the earth—
—landing is a motion, an encounter, a trial, a balancing attempt.

How we learn and relearn to speak to our own body. To say— this way, in this direction. To tell our senses, which see no ground, that our grounding is elsewhere.

It is this faith in small acts that helps us envision our own directionality.

Why all this now? Now as we are unmoored, enclosed, and flailing simultaneously. Our usual footholds have fallen away. Our springboards are absent. There are no familiar buttons to help us navigate this unknown ship—small craft comprised of walls and the few people in our household. Each time we go out, we can't know what to expect. The way we once learned to hold our bodies in public spaces serves us no anchor now.

19

Cynthia Alessandra Briano

We have to relearn how to move, where to put our hands, how to navigate public space with our bodies, how to hold our own bodies far enough from the intimacy of each other.

Even at home, our bodies are not at rest any longer. We can't sleep. The space has changed—the whole of our world has been compressed into it. Time is a new stretch that plunges or escapes us. Its immensity finally felt in its unknowable dimensions—how long will this last? How long has it been? Will I be able to withstand?

And the motion of our hands—we have to relearn to use our hands.

The way we move through this time is only through the minutiae of movement—making dinner, washing our hands, laying our bodies down, not to sleep—we have lost that anchor—but to fall. Each night we learn to fall over and over again. First in the freefall of fear, of uncertainty in the dark, and no one can help you. Even if you share a bed, each one of us must navigate the freefall alone: how to steady our fear, how to steady our core from the outside in.

How to make the decision to navigate your own fall? Each night we learn and relearn it, though it is not the same leap. Each night, the band that encloses our being is still elastic, still capable of careening. Each night, the body is finally responsive—it succumbs to its own balance and counterbalance. Each night, we choose a small light in the distance and cantilever our fear against our faith. But the next star is always far away.

Donny Jackson

antebellum

it's how i keep time is the answer

i don't know when i wake up whose birth certificate is on fire
or if they are already in bright colors on a wall on my block or
in my feed but i know like everybody else how the roster
became a metronome and certainly this is my new heartbeat
which says i am now more machine than human and
remember we were taught that what machines do is allow the
work of humans to be easier and isn't that how this all started
in the first place except instead of the plantation being real
estate run by tyrants who impregnate the help it's the idea
that my tick is silent which allows the work of people who
think they know me to be easier yet nothing about the
landscape tells anyone i know how much harder it is for me to
savor how my right hand used to be a lost language on your
left cheek the last native speaker and we didn't care that every
poem we said unloud would perish with us

quietly

not even counted among the dead

Juan Delgado

El Dorado

I.
When we had a kitchen counter to start
our morning and a Yucca pot to water
and ease our worries of the approaching fire,
we had the urgency of facing the notices to evacuate together.

A voice hovered, swooping down
into our canyon with deafening blades.
We wore our masks in the car, driving out of the canyon;
a tree line of smoke and bursts of fire escorted us out.

At a crosswalk, the nakedness of a house door fazed us.

II.
Our staircase was a reminder of pending routines;
our bed pillows were not properly fluffed up
and put back in their dream spots.
Though we left our house under daylight,
the gas pilots were still blue eyed, ready for dinner.
In a glance, the hinges froze, doors half-closed.
The living room drapes touched the floor,
making their shadows widen.
In their cup, yellow pencils pointed up,
too dull for words.

Juan Delgado

III.

We learned the ways of interpreting maps. *Are we on the other
side of that ridge? Is that where we live? There. There. Is that it?* In
a rented room, we fixated on containment lines while a finger
pressed down on a hotspot as if to erase it. When we double-
checked the door lock and fell into our single beds, we asked
what remained in the side view mirror. We were occupied
with the topography of tongues in full spirit and their
ambition to spread north. Outside our window and on the
well-lit parking lot, the storytellers repeated themselves over
the radio. And a car slept by the glow of a half-smoked
cigarette.

IV.

They say the fire has a gender,
but it needs no one, refusing any single face.
It's inexorable, breeding, dormant at times
while living in us and beyond us
like an economy of consuming. Especially
at night, its self-made winds
push up against us, and though we tire,
the fire never loses its breath to remind us
where we truly are.

Terri Niccum

When you haven't any choice, make one

When they came for our lupines,
we acted embarrassed. We hadn't planted any.
We had only echeverias, agaves
and a few kangaroo paws, and those
only had two red buds. It had been
a hard year for plants. Hence
the government's need to gather bloomers
for Tyrant Baby. And he wanted blue
blossoms to set off his orange hair.
The suits with guns tramped through our yard
and then tramped through our house
in case we were concealing. Then
they confiscated our tablets and
revoked our viewing privileges.
No great loss really.
Ever since the last election
there has been very little to watch
except for the weekly streaming of
Tyrant Baby trimming his toenails.
They gave us a packet of lupine seeds
and demanded *Get planting!*
We made with the motions
until the suits had gone.
Then we doubled over
in silent laughter, remembering the days
when it was ok to laugh out loud.

Terri Niccum

We went inside
and held each other
which also is illegal, but we still did it.
We washed the lupine seeds down the drain,
dug into a drawer and found two old packets
of Mexican Primrose seeds.
Outside in the newly churned earth
we planted those hopeful kernels,
envisioning pink petals
like flags ruffling the wind.

Steve Ramirez

After the Aliens Landed, They Had Questions

Once they stopped laughing
at what we call technology,
of course.

They tried to hide it
but the one in back
(the one we thought
of as Kevin)--

it's always a Kevin, isn't it?
--he kept chuckling whenever
one of our scientists--
oh, please, Kevin laughed,
you call this science?

you can't even draw a straight line
between your own greed and global warming!

Our scientists tried to explain that greed has nothing to do with science.
see?

The aliens asked us about everything;
healthcare   *it has nothing to do with either of those words*
the economy   *it sounds like a game of keep away*
religion   *you hate each other over what happens after you die*

Steve Ramirez

Strangely, what confused them most--
what they kept asking about--was our phones.

How we stare at these little pools of light in our palms.
How we frame each other through these tiny windows.
How convenient, turning the world on and off with the push of a button.

Earlier in the day, there had been a school shooting.
I don't remember which one. After all, aliens landed,
and this is America, our children get shot at every day.

Devourers

It writhed on the crumbling stone dais. All inky black feelers, glistening with some primordial slime.

Faint light from above filtered down through the ruins. Ancient stonework had faded over the centuries in this almost-forgotten world. A man spoke faintly into a palm-sized device, the lights a steady pulse in the dark. His heart beat steady.

"No life signs, as expected."

The thing on the dais jolted, but otherwise did not seem to move from its position.

The man carefully walked around it. "Matches descriptions and theoretical behavior." He paused. "Protrusions do not appear to be tentacles." He raised the device and held it straight in front of him, as if for the inky slime to speak its secrets. After a moment, he let his arm drop. "Recording complete. Observations done. Confirmation of one-hundred thirty-seven theories so far."

He pulled a flat pad from a pack on the ground, reading the contents. He took no chances, sending today's findings to his ship. Many of the legends and rumors were true: the thing was deadly, dangerous, and would not bend to inquiry easily. But he had prepared.

Stepping back, he took the bag and placed all the devices he had into the pack. The thing stopped writhing and instead formed a complex sculpture in the dais, as if some ancient hands hand molded and encouraged it to grow that way. It pulsed.

"Marvelous," the man said. He grabbed a piece of parchment and a bit of coal and began a crude sketch.

It made no sound, nor acknowledgement of his presence. After a few more minutes, he tucked the parchment under his arm and turned to leave the chamber.

hunger

The man stopped and turned around, unnerved. The thing no longer rested on the dais as a sculpture. It had flowed from the stone into grooves set on the ground. He pulled out the recording device. "More a feeling than a word."

Inky blackness shivered and writhed again.

"It reacts to the recorder in the same way."

hunger

Its writhing pulled it closer to the man. He had backed away, but still kept his eyes on the creature.

hungerhungerhunger

"More voices?" He spun around. Black, glistening ooze surrounded him. More than he had seen on the dais just moments ago. They seemed more attracted in their writhing than repulsed. He shoved everything in the pack, save a small trinket he attached to his belt.

The man disappeared. The writing slowed. Stopped.

hunger

Rubble far down the corridor to the enormous chamber shifted and settled.

Blood rushed through the man's veins. There had been no evidence of previous exploration. No remains of anyone from the civilization found. One more theory to add, to prove.

Terri Niccum

Different

What's different now is that every time
you close our front door, you think
It might be the last time. The last
time you go out, the last time
you come back in. A life of looking back
over your shoulder, reassessing
wrong moves, is no life. We don't need
this life of second guessing. I don't want to be
your second guess. And we can't even see
our pursuer with the invisibility cloak, the one
who would lodge inside us, set us flaring,
steal our breath.

I have looked and looked
and I can't find the spell to undo this.
My magic loses its way in this dark place.
But out of long habit, I hand you my heart
like a rune. You rub it like a bottle
and let me out!

Come dance with me, Love!
This is a new dance, we make up the steps.
Take my hands that are only bones
but become hands again with your touch.
You have no shoes but on your feet
my eyes paint silver boots.

Terri Niccum

Dance! like your body never could
but your soul always longed to.
Well, now you can.
Dance, and if we move our feet like rotors,
our sweetly entwined feet,
we find ourselves lifting
above the chimneys, above the roofs.
And this is how we leave, Love,
because nothing is coming back,
and we must fill our empty pockets
with the new.
Look into my eyes
and let me introduce you.
This is who we become.

Burt Shultz

the world will end
with the mutterings of
a madman

When This is Over

I want to drive across the country.

I want to sleep in motel rooms whose windows open onto the interstate.

I want to listen to FM radio,
to Willie Nelson, John Lee Hooker, Grand Funk Railroad,
Bonnie Raitt, Kacey Musgraves, & Don Henley.

I want to pull into a drive-in theater somewhere in the Midwest
& watch Michelle Rodriguez & Vin Diesel drive cars
at impossibly high rates of speed.

I want to drink Coca Cola, fresh-squeezed lemonade,
cheap beer, & cold water.

I want to eat in fast food joints where the young woman
at the counter daydreams through my entire order

about the life she's going to have once she graduates from college,
or saves some money, or falls in love, or wins the lottery.

I want to pray in churches whose marquees
say that "God is Love", that "Jesus Saves", that "Kindness is Mercy."

I want to get a sunburn.

Kareem Tayyar

I want to dance in the rain.

I want to shake hands with the mechanic
who fixes my car when it breaks down on Highway 61,
or Route 66, or the Blue Ridge Parkway.

I want to slow-dance with a woman I meet
in a roadside bar when I am too tired to drive any further,

my hands around her waist, her hands around my neck,
her breath in my ear, my heart in my throat.

I want to swim in rivers whose names I don't recognize.

I want to sit in the stands of baseball stadiums
with thousands of strangers

& cheer for the slugger to hit one out,

for the runner to reach home, for the game to go extra innings.

I want to hear live music.

I want to go to Mardi Gras.

I want to see New York City again.

I want to see Chicago for the very first time.

Donny Jackson

corona, 1555–65
latin: corōna garland, crown; greek: korónē crown, curved object;
akin to korōnís: curved, beaked, kórax: crow, raven.

it is 34 degrees and white sky in quinhagak alaska
and not one of the 700 townspeople
the first of this land
is thinking about toilet paper
or hand sanitizer
or a check from what they do not call government
because
tribal police said
ida aguchak
10
stopped being missing
in a dump
and now she will only ever be 10
and her hands
newborn chickadees
full of chirp
as they waved
are still and more alaska now than girl and
the first person to pick her up is doomed
to not be able to put her down
forever and
someone
is bound to ask

Donny Jackson

if it was a hunter from outside or
if the town eats its young

and this is the only virus in the village
and everyone
has already died from it
a black bird over the town
no one can see

and in the 48 states connected by theft before this one
ida aguchak
10
is just another of the many words we don't know
for snow

Julia Ingalls

Elevator Music

If solitude is standing on a rugged plateau, overlooking miles of wilderness, then isolation is getting stuck in a tiny windowless elevator between floors. In any other year aside from 2020 getting stuck in such an elevator would be unusual, or at least easily remedied: but the maintenance staff are corrupt, the building itself is likely to fall down, and when we press the help button all we can hear are each other's electronically-warped laments.

It has been hard to have a party in here. Safety issues are paramount, of course, but the real obstacle comes in the fact that my friends fall on the side of sanity, which is to say they don't want to infect or be infected with the virus. There have only been a few instances this year in which I was able to truly feel like a part of humanity, as I used to in the safe air days: one of these, a masked-up Black Lives Matter protest marching down Washington Boulevard about a week after the death of George Floyd, was powerful, profound, and healing.

The other involved a spontaneous grocery store dance party.

Because I am healthy and believe that app-based delivery services tend only to monetarily benefit the app-makers at the expense of everyone else, I have become something of a grocery store connoisseur, which is to say I now classify grocery stores based not on their food offerings but rather on their ambiance. Most Ralph's are frightening: the aisles are both too tall and skinny, making it easy to get trapped in the middle while on either end seemingly oblivious cart-pushers thunder toward you with likely contagion. Sprouts has a luxurious open plan design, but the employees have that kind of listless, beaten quality that tells me that management probably doesn't treat them well. Trader Joe's, despite its long lines, has the benefit of camaraderie: everyone working, and shopping there seems to value the preservation of each other's health, which makes it less like a lethal treasure hunt and more like an old-fashioned trip to the grocery store.

In any case, after the initial shock of the pandemic wore off and everyone lucky enough to be alive began to realize that our existences were going to be indefinitely constrained, other factors started to weigh upon me. For instance, the soundtrack in Trader Joe's, which previously had seemed light, upbeat, even perhaps cheering in a cheesy way, now seemed cruel and tone-deaf. I remember forcing myself not to punch anything as "I'm Walking on Sunshine" blared out on the overhead speakers. Each visit became a weird aural torture session: all the hits of the retrospectively carefree decades before us, bringing up memories that now seemed to taunt us with impossibility.

The change came one afternoon in late July, during surging case numbers and deaths. I walked down near-vacant streets to my local Trader Joe's, thinking about insects trapped in amber. I entered the store after getting the all clear from the person out front and headed toward the frozen aisle. There, as I stared desultorily at the cheese tamales, a familiar but not immediately identifiable few bars of synthesizer pulsed out from the speakers. It felt as though everyone in the store stopped what they were doing and really tuned in: what was this song? The melody repeated, and holding our positions, we all began to spontaneously bop and groove.

By necessity, the motions were small. The woman near the packaged fruit tapped out the beat with her left heel. A man pushing a cart nodded his head. When we reached the instrumental chorus of "Axel F," the theme from "Beverly Hills Cop," I saw some robot-like pop-and-lock shoulder rolls. Again, nothing that would encroach on each other, but enough so that we could all see, we could all participate. No one had to say anything, but there was the sense we were all smiling under our masks.

Unlike the other pop hits turned torture devices, "Axel F" felt more contemporary. Yes, its synthesizers seemed to say, there's danger out there. But there's also a little room for fun. And, perhaps crucially, it didn't tell us about how it was addicted to love or that it was working for the weekend or that it was a sledgehammer. It just let us dance together, for three perfectly socially distanced minutes.

Donna Hilbert

A Burning Somewhere

On Sunday, I snap a dazzling sunset photo
of the golden orb plummeting to the sea.
At first, I think my dirty window is the only filter:
panes glazed by offshore winds and coastal fog.
Then, I realize it's the flames
in inland foothills, canyons, desert flatlands
that have rendered blue skies umber.
Slater, Lone Star, Creek, Bobcat, El Dorado,
to name a blazing few.
Death is the mother of beauty, the poet claims.
Does this hold true?
Always, a burning, always a fire.
Somewhere a hearth, somewhere a pyre.

The italicized line is from "Sunday Morning," by Wallace
Stevens

Arminé Iknadossian

Dear Morning After Lockdown Week 25:

dear shadow of skylark on concrete
dear friend who sends me water colors of the sea
dear sister I send you this recipe for sourdough

oh the precious distance
oh the sinful wish
dear uncle, dear auntie, dear so and so

take my guilt as wide as my hips
take the weight of our cities
sagging into their sad harbors

dear morning, it is now afternoon,
so sudden, how time flies in this stillness
of worry, in this worried stillness

in this year of our lord have mercy

Dare Williams

Hyper Vigilance

Middle of the night mom wakes me up
from my seven-year old bed, frantic.

Big ideas pour out of her mouth
an avalanche of thoughts.
She turns on every light
and flutters from room to room.

I travel down the hall
to find her in the kitchen, making a plan.

I don't do anything because
the plan isn't real.

I watch her inhale between statements
tapping her cigarette like a wand
ash peppers the sink.

She wipes the counters while
the room fills with smoke and panic

a balloon about to burst.

My mother's pain is a tree that has fallen
through the house
something to walk around
but not remove.

Dare Williams

*

Tonight, at thirty-eight
choppers grinding the dark
wake me up
windows hum to a growled tempo.

My mother was not a helicopter parent.

Spotlights search the city
filling my apartment in pale white
bombs in the alley flash their stink
a loud march swells to off-key strings.

I leave my body while I pace.

I think of what might need to come with me
mom in my head yelling,

We have to go we have to go
We have to go we have to go.

Kevin Ridgeway

This Poem Kills Fascism

the President forgot
how to be smart
a long time ago,
before he was even born
to be a digitized tyrant
and impatient, insolent
and pathetic king baby
who has already fucked
things up enough for us to have
days darker in the orange smog
of brush fires lit by lazy minded
demonic mad-headed
power trippers like him
who have no attention span
and are more aggressive
than WWF wrestlers
from hell who declare
revenge on America for failing
to be great again
and for giving us
all of these fucking cooties
we are trying to vote
out of office so we can
make America better
than it ever was before

Kevin Ridgeway

on the tired backs
of my grandparents
who sacrificed everything
during the depression
to raise their kids
face to weary face
with a fascism
they killed back then
and we will kill
that fascism again
with a hope that's
bound for glory at last

Stephanie Barbé Hammer

Yadaim

It's a Jewish thing. The ritual washing of the hands.

You have resisted it, because it happens at an awkward moment on *Shabbat*. Everyone is assembled for the Friday night feast or the Saturday luncheon. You're about to eat bread, but instead -- you have to get up, and if you're at an Orthodox Shabbat table, you have to line up behind a whole crew of people and wait your turn at the kitchen sink. It's all very public. There is nothing private about praying in Judaism. And what makes it potentially embarrassing is that the ritual involves complex acts of water-pouring from a two-handled cup. three pours over the left and three over the right. Or perhaps it's just two (*remember*, your tell yourself, *this is Judaism and not Christianity with its preoccupation with 3's*), and perhaps it's right hand, left hand. You're still not sure.

You're a convert. So you still tend to make things three when they're two or seven or ten or eighteen.

And for a while you couldn't remember the word for "hands" in Hebrew.

The word is *yad*; plural is *yadaim*; it's the same word used for the little stick that the rabbi uses to scan the lines of the *Torah*. No physical fingers should touch the parchment, because it is so delicate and hard to make.

You met a *sofer* – a biblical scribe – last year in Jerusalem, and he went into detail about the practice of writing down

Torah, the prayers when you get to the end of a section. He said he loved the process of transcription.

Eventually your attitude towards the handwashing changed, though. You learned – from someone – that the handwashing ritual was originally a priestly act, reserved for the *Kohanim* in Temples one and two in Jerusalem. When the Second Temple fell, the priestly order faded away, although it was not destroyed as anyone named Cohen will tell you (they're the official priestly descendants). But certain practices were passed on and conferred, not just to men, but even to women and children. This is surprising, given the patriarchal roots of Judaism – of the big three monotheisms in general. Now, every person can become a priest in that instant of standing at the sink.

These days, the practice overflows with meaning. Everyone is – at least for a moment – not just Jewish, but Orthodox, and not just Orthodox, but a pontiff, washing and washing before any activity that involves touching your face.

"Isn't it interesting," the young female rabbi said on Zoom during Passover. "How ancient people already understood the difference between clean and unclean? Already knew that purification was crucial?"

You're not so crazy for this interpretation, because women traditionally – in every culture just about – have been regarded as problematic, purity-wise. People in need of frequent cleaning. And of course this Reconstructionist woman rabbi wouldn't even be considered a rabbi by the Orthodox Jews in your own family!

But now everyone is equally tainted. There is finally some equality in this strange moment of danger and potential transformation.

"We are," this same young woman rabbi reminds the congregation, "a nation of priests."

What about a continent of priests? A world of priests? Wouldn't that be something? A global citizenship of people actively blessing each other.

You nod, turn the tap. Right hand, left hand. Soap. Rinse. Dry. You speak the prayer. It couldn't hurt. But you don't eat right now. You sit at the computer instead. The word for "writer" in Hebrew is also *sofer*. The feminine is *soferet*. Your fingers sit with it, waiting to transcribe.

Alexandra Umlas

Wild Dust (Or, What I Tell Myself During Lockdown)
—after Mary Oliver

You do not have to wash your sheets.
You do not have to button back the comforter
for an hour in your dark bedroom, tired.
You only have to let the quiet night
slip around the stars.
Tell me about your filth, yours, and I will tell you mine.
Meanwhile everything gets dirtier.
Meanwhile the dishes still appear in the sink
stuck with food-glue, the tub ring grows more opaque,
your socks disappear one by one into who knows,
never to be seen again.
Meanwhile your lungs, tucked into your warm body,
are expanding again.
Whoever you are, no matter how grimy,
the body offers itself as an example,
sticks to you like the wild dust, silky and falling—
over and over creating you a soft place
in the unwashed splendor of things.

Brendan Constantine

Wave Diary, March 19, 2020

The virus waved at me today   from across
the street.   It was carrying bags of food
and shapes I couldn't guess.   I waved back,
tried to smile.   Come over, it shouted,
I have extra masks   and this water won't
drink itself.   Another time, I called back,
my hands to my face.   Yes, it answered,
another time.

Donna Hilbert

Clean

Mother rinsed dishes in a mix
of hot water and bleach,
and, with the same noxious brew,
swabbed door knobs and faucets.
Not even latches on gates escaped
her everyday war on disease.
That was before we knew
what plague lay in wait
to smite us and lock us in place.
Wherever you are, beyond the urn
in my closet, Mother, hear me concede:
you were right when you told me
a girl must be careful,
and *there's no such thing as too clean*

Terri Niccum

Winter's Weight

The sky leans on leaves, finding itself
too heavy to hold up, buried

like me, missing sunlight but
clinging to fog, reaching for my cup, buried.

Her muffler, muffling dreams,
hides beneath socks, wool-nubbed and gruff, buried.

Six pall bearers, black-suited shoulders slumped over
the doll-sized box two could have carried; child interrupted,
buried

and afterwards, the unspoken days
smothered with ashes and accusations, joy corrupted, buried.

Still, your leaving was like a train; scheduled whistle,
soot and steam – chop stump abrupt, buried.

Years spend, that story's faded, bits of rag
nibbled by the wind, inhaled like a favorite snuff, buried.

If winter is a bulb deep in earth,
Terri, shake the rattle, scatter seed and dust, wake up
the buried.

Take a Pause

One week after California issued its stay-at-home order, I turned to a friend and asked, "Why can't we all just take a pause?"

Wouldn't it be helpful if we took a week – hell, even a few days off – to collect ourselves? We are in the middle of a global pandemic. We were told this information well after our government knew about it, and our distrust in them will only continue to grow over the next few months. Rather than take a moment to process what this all means for our day to day and figure out how we will keep ourselves and our loved ones safe, we are instructed to keep grinding hard at work, to virtually ignore the world around us, or at least to not let it affect our relationship with productivity.

During the first two months of quarantine, my Parent Friends were forced to work alongside their spouses and children, to teach their children geometry even though they hated it when they were in school, and were humbled by the sheer workload the average public school teacher puts in each week.

Meanwhile, my Friends Who Live Alone were facing low-grade depression, anxiety, insomnia, an unhealthy relationship with social media, the need to learn to cook basic meals for themselves, a gratitude for Netflix, and if enormously lucky, a family home to escape to "until it is over."

My Essential Worker Friends include those who work for the United States Postal Service, oncologists who treat at-risk cancer patients, and my 16-year-old neighbor who works as a cashier at the local Ralph's (she said she is just trying to save money for college and is happy for the overtime).

My Newly Unemployed Friends include Parents, Single Friends Who Live Alone, Couples Who Share Tiny Spaces, and Non-Essential Workers. Many have just witnessed the local business they work for collapse overnight. They've spent hours on hold or online, attempting to find the appropriate paperwork so they could have food on the table. People who historically didn't "believe" in unemployment benefits had sacrificed their convictions to stand first in line to get a handout, a helping hand.

My Queer Trans Black Indigenous People of Color Friends watched as the world shouted with conviction, "BLACK LIVES MATTER!" We continue to watch as the BLM movement is met with arguments that all lives – that blue lives – matter, too. And we all take a collective sigh at a missed point. Our fellow Black Americans watch as people that look like them are murdered, their deaths recorded and shared on social media, only to then be questioned on their goodness, their lawfulness, while the officers who kill them walk free in the same city where families of the victims want answers, want justice.

This is not new – it did not start in 2020. This is in the history of this nation. And yet, even when the Human Rights Commission declared racism a public health crisis, when the very soul of our nation is up for grabs to white supremacists, we are asked to keep grinding. We are instructed not to take a pause. The economy just cannot withstand that kind of loss. Loss. What then of the lives that have been stolen? No pause for those losses? No reverence, no reflection, no soul.

Forced productivity is as American as apple pie, but no amount of whipped cream can disguise the obvious mistakes of our government. If we are being told to keep grinding away, how and when can we take a pause?

The first thing to realize is that we cannot wait until our employers or families or spouses give us permission to take a pause. We must take it ourselves and use the energy it gives us to help others if we are so able.

So while we are busy trying to maintain job security, raise our children, not fall into a deep depression – in what small ways can we take a pause for ourselves?

For me, in no specific order of importance, I have observed or personally experienced these varying kinds of pause:

Practicing daily morning meditation. Reading before falling asleep. Binge-watching four episodes of the *Great British Bake Off*. Meal prepping. Ordering carryout instead. Finally picking up that bass guitar. Holding solo dance parties while stress cleaning the entire apartment. These are pauses.

Baking banana bread. Making a sourdough starter. Googling, "Is this sourdough starter supposed to smell like a dirty gym sock?" Hitting the snooze button when you need to. Waking up fifteen minutes before work starts and walking to your desk half asleep. Sun Salutations each morning.

Sleeping an hour into your workday and nobody notices. Quitting your day job, moving to the mountains of Colorado, and writing from your newly purchased tiny home. These are also pauses.

Going for a daily walk or run or, zombied-level exhausted, float through your neighborhood. Taking breaks between work assignments. Taking a "quick" three-hour nap before clocking out for the day. Scheduling video chat dates with friends across the country. Getting too tired from Zooming all day at work and rescheduling the video chat date. Being exceptionally compassionate to friends experiencing burnout. Talking to that one friend you love but haven't seen in years for hours. Promising to talk again. Never talking again. Texting your ex.

Taking the weekend away from social media. Taking a weekend to decide how you will help fight the racial injustices of this country, this world. Realizing it's gonna take a helluva lot more than reading anti-racist books over a patriotic holiday weekend to be an anti-racist. Quoting Nipsey, "It's a marathon, not a sprint." Understanding that and being willing, still, to do the work. Being really comfortable wearing dolphin shorts all day. Getting dressed up and doing your makeup just to enjoy a nice dinner alone on your balcony or with someone you really love.

To All My Different Types of Friends, you deserve a pause. How will you take yours?

Breakout Rooms	Room 1
Breakout /breâk'out'/ adj. denoting to groups that break away from a conference for discussion. n. An outbreak. A categorized list. A forceful break from a restrictive condition or situation. A sudden advance to a new level.	Muted beginners stare at each other's faces to investigate adolescent breakouts.
Room 2	**Room 3**
Clicks on Oryx & Crake for instructions. Lost learner fails to find the passage, ends up in a high school Calculus class in China. Starts at the intersection of virus & white supremacy. Catches the 405, takes Facebook Blvd leading to the 110 Instagram-bound at rush hour, connects to the 91 East, exits on the YouTube ramp.	Intermediate leaners practice breaking out bad news to each other. You are not an essential worker. Your job has been terminated. Your unemployment benefits will expire next week. You are an essential worker, but we don't have a PE for you. You've been evicted. We are out of toilet paper. Your class doesn't have enough students to keep it open.

Room 4	Room 5
Advanced learners practice delivering good news: Uncle Donald contracted an orange strain of COVID19. We inserted the ventilator in his rear end. We had to. He signed the consent form, "dropped his pants and touched his toes." We washed our hands for twenty seconds afterwards.	Learners out of emotional tools, wearing face masks, break out in sweat & palpitations, afraid of another pandemic breakout stemming from experimental vaccine rushed too soon before the elections.
Room 6	**Room 7**
Aggravated learners demand to preview an exit route out of this horror of daily shootings, bigots carrying AR-15 roam streets, refusing to wear masks, coughing on store clerks. Homeland Security shooting rubber pellets at point-blank to peaceful protesters, Black men unable to breathe under the weight of law-enforced lynching, KKK dressed in blue.	Surprised learner finds that the pandemic is her breakout room. Digs a hole in the floor with a plastic spoon, covers it during the faculty check-ins, and uses it to escape from the prison she has built for herself. She crawls out in a bright orange jumpsuit catching the attention of ex-felons and wardens alike, in this postapocalyptic year 2020 of red skies and ash rain, drive-by funerals, and fires induced by gender-reveal parties.
Room 8	
Committed leaner advances to next level, discovers this is her chance to shine, when the stars dim in the confinement she knows too well. Forgets to click JOIN	

James Evert Jones

Inkwell

Minorities do not believe they are minorities
because most everyone in the world is in color.
The title was thrust upon them, much like royalty
and, as royalty does, grief is magnified
when someone dies. A eulogy is written
to speak to the lessening, to tame the remaining void.

The writer taps his mind for a way to keep writing.

Minorities, like royalty, possess tribes of raconteurs
who celebrate life with us; lament loss with us
from acts progressively cruel and inventive –
a knee on the neck, a plastic bag about the face.
Parents caution children to regard the phantom laws
that lead to moonlight scythes from midnight reapers
and televised keening. The parched author's inkwell
foments a notion. He whittles the barrel to an obtuse angle.

The writer taps a vein so he can keep writing.

Minorities do not believe they warrant execution
for the exhilarating lush of their pigment or its by-products:
the cursive of their walk, speech, dance, sex, song.
The constant violence is thrust upon them, like a coup.
A welling of red gums his fingers, the crook of his elbow,
his works become a dusty coagulant; the hand fails – fails.

The writer tapped a vein so he could keep writing
and his pen, they will say, caused his death.

Brian Harman

20/20 Vision

20 feet from the Snellen eye chart,
line 8 used to be clear;
D E F P O T E C,
recitable as Aretha Franklin's
R E S P E C T—
come to find out
in the actual year 2020,
what it means to not have
clear vision anymore;
outside of my newborn
and the love of my inner circle,
it means
locked up in an air full
of smoke and mirrors,
it means
faculties of labyrinth,
oligarch roulette,
it means
search for higher ground within,
sight of now, slight of future,
flight of Icarus,
Phoenix start all over again,
top line, E,
second line, F P,
third line, T O Z,
fourth line, L P E D,
fifth, I don't know,
R E S P E—
but I don't believe in hope.

Ben Trigg

Purpose

*"if you can remove a female character from your plot and replace her
with a sexy lamp and your story still works, you're a hack."*
—Kelly Sue DeConnick

Put the fruit down. Don't offer him a bite.
He will be happier in ignorance.
You knew this about him before your own teeth tore
into fleshy knowledge.
Don't pretend you were tricked. You could already feel
the divide.
He was content with doing the naming.
Of course he was, it gave him purpose.
Your purpose was to look pretty while he did things.
A sexy lamp, if you will.

Understanding looks better on you than your spotlight ever
looked on him.

Fred Voss

Janis Joplin Never Belted Southern Comfort Bourbon and Screamed the Blues

"We've got to wear these fricking masks!"
says our new supervisor
to us machinists and de-burrers and shipping clerks and
    punch press operators gathered
around him on the shop floor for the special coronavirus
pandemic meeting he has called
to tell us we must all wear our sanitary masks at all times
he says "fricking"
instead of "fucking"
because long since the days when he was a hippie
and said "fucking" in every other sentence
he quit drugs
and drinking and blasting iconoclastic long-haired-hippie
    rock music and joined
a fundamentalist Christian church
and started saying "fricking" instead of "fucking"
"fucking"
sounds earthy and solid and true and sexy and noble
as an elephant trumpeting
a steamroller rolling
a Hula dancer swaying her hips under a Waikiki palm tree
Freud uncovering a repressed memory
Joe Louis landing a k.o. punch to Max Schmeling's Nazi jaw
"fricking"

sounds like something that would make Jimi Hendrix
unplug his electric guitar
Romeo forget Juliet Harry Houdini
resign himself to handcuffs Valentino take off his tango shoes
    Jim Morrison
put on a hair shirt
and the supervisor finishes by telling us to all wear our masks
    at all times and stay
in good health and then shouts,
"Alright! Let's all get back to fricking work!"
would Paul Bunyan
have said "fricking"
would that speeding locomotive driver Casey Jones would
    Jack Dempsey Pablo Picasso
Janis Joplin never belted Southern Comfort bourbon and
    screamed the blues
Lead Belly never split a chain-gang boulder with a
    sledgehammer
and we machinists and shipping clerks and de-burrers and
    punch press operators
file back toward our machines
as all the air goes out of all the balloons
on earth

Something like a pandemic that's a matter of global life and death
ought to at least make men give
a fuck.

Shana Nicholson-Morgan

Cracking

Give us this day our daily bread.

"Tina. I had such a good idea, babe. If Vatican City started making homemade baby food they could call the business 'Pope Purée'. Get it?"

Weigh the flour and water precisely. Mix well. Then, the flour needs to be left alone to hydrate.

I stare at him like I want to punch him directly in his Adam's apple. No, not *like* I want to punch him in his Adam's apple. I genuinely, literally, actually want to punch him in his Adam's apple.

Sprinkle salt. Add yeast. Mix the dough using your hands as the tools they're meant to be. Stretch it to the point of breaking, then fold the orb in on itself by pulling the warm dough from the bottom up and over the top. Cut and fold again. Feel the mass tensing up in your hands with each action.

"Do I have to even tell you, Dan, why the Catholic church and a venture involving kids may not thrive?"

Take care not to let the dough get overly warm or too cool. Cover the pale moon-shape and let it rise. After a while fold the dough again. This is important to strengthening the framework of its structure.

"Fucking hell? Why are my good pans all banged up, Dan?"

"I used them last night when I went on the balcony to thank the health care workers."

"Goddammit! These are Calphalon!"

If you listen closely you might hear the yeast multiplying. This is what it is to bake - to have a feel for the unseen. Soon, it will be time to stretch and fold again. This time make note of the tension. Add flour to the surface to prevent it from getting stuck. Half it. Shape. Proof.

"T, Have you given any more thought to the sitcom idea I had? The one about conjoined twins? One's an alt-right blogger and the other is chief-of-staff for Alexandra Ocasio-Cortez?"

Bake the loaves on the middle rack. Make sure to preheat the oven first so the bread knows what it's getting itself into. Let it do what it needs to do. Be patient. Take them out when they're brown, but not too brown. It's been a process. Let them rest.

"Okay how about this? I pitch a reality show with me and you. It's called 'QuaranTina'."

Listen to the loaves crack as they cool.

Cut into it with your best knife. The shattering crust and steam release has been well-earned. Take a bite and give no thought to the crumbs tumbling on top of your bare feet and onto the cold kitchen floor.

Ra Avis

Humanwatch

A lizard crawls along the hot pavement and drinks the sky in quick flickering laps. Greedy is okay today. No humans are outside, and the sky is big enough to fill her stomach many times over.

The light is too hot for the palm trees, so the wind cools them-- deep focused breaths of crisp air rattling their fronds. There's no wind on the ground. The temperature is just right for those of us who can move our slumberous bodies.

My own body hasn't gone outside in some time. From the second floor, I press myself against the window and watch the streets. They are still, steady, sun-basked, gossiping with the clouds. They can whisper today because the sounds of engines and footsteps are finally gone.

My entire apartment is filled with light, and I see dust bunnies in a corner just swept. How many other things hide in the cover of darkness, surviving our reaches and work?

There is no hiding for me in my home. It fishtanks out to a bustling city, and if anything about me was a secret before the morning came, it wouldn't be now.

On the rooftop of a shop across the way, a bird lands. His mouth opens wide and he eats at the sun, gulping it into his belly. He watches me the whole time, and then flies away without ever saying hello.

Ra Avis

I do not know what type of bird he is.

In the wind, alongside birdchatter, I can hear other humans crying out, a keening but near-silent call.

I answer it.
I have to.

I know what type of human I am.

Arminé Iknadossian

11th Hour
—*after Dean Young's "Zero Hour"*

Like the moment you realized as a child
that the sunrise is not your mother's face.
With your small fingers, what did you understand
about impressionists and their landscapes?
Some day you will realize that old paint cracks
on canvas; the artist has little control of this.
We can fix the engines in our cars,
bleach the grout in the bathroom,
and still suffer from our fever dream.
It's easy for body to pull itself away from spirit.
It's cooler without, opaque and unhaunted.
The trees are sinking, the clouds are rocks,
the water line recedes to reveal ancient handprints.
It is certain the pre-party ended too soon.
We emptied our platters, overwatered the ferns.
Everything entered daylight as if it always could.

Fred Voss

Evolution Deniers and Dinosaur Bone Collectors

I wish they could have a psychologist's office in each factory
when machinists are hired
they would immediately go into the psychologist's office to
    take a complete battery
of psychological tests
no longer
would an atheist who believes there is no meaning to
    anything be put on a machine
next to the machine of a man who likes to tape quotes from
    the Bible
to the walls
a man who wants to start a whorehouse in El Salvador
would be put on the opposite side of the shop from a man
    who loves his wife
and family above all else
men who circle their machines spouting X-rated rap lyrics at
    high volume
or whistling ear-piercing off-key corny songs from bad
    movies all day
will no longer spend their workdays with their shoulders five
    feet from the shoulders of men
who love to play Mozart on a violin
a pacifist Buddhist
no longer have to look close up all day into the eyes
of a rabid National Rifle Association member
we give machinists we interview for jobs math and blueprint-
    reading tests

Fred Voss

isn't the mental health and happiness
of men who have to work together for 20 or 30 years as important
as how well they can square up
a block of steel
or how fast they can bolt a 100-pound vise to a machine table
shouldn't two men
who love nothing better than camping out in the mountains
     looking for rocks to add
to their rock collections get the chance to work at machines next
to each other for years
and when a man is trembling inside with rage all day because
     the man
at the next machine has been needling
him for 20 years to see if he can make him crack shouldn't
he have a psychologist's office to walk into before
he pulls out a gun
Trump enthusiasts
next to democratic socialists evolution deniers
next to men who love to hike the desert hunting for dinosaur
     bones
isn't there a better way
should men who carve steel with their bare hands all their
     lives to make this world
have to drive each other crazy
living in it?

Arthur Kayzakian

Dear Cyrus,

My time in isolation has been buried in books. The more I read, the more reluctant I am to speak. When I open a book, my body turns into a candle set aflame. I am having trouble naming things, and now in my small grasp of time, I have been thinking about my name etched on my birth certificate, or the one engraved on my citizenship. I have one of those new ones with the fancy holographic signature. When I wave the document left to right, a metallic proof of residency spangles under a web of lights. Some immigration scholars would argue the way a name is scratched on immigration papers suggests a printed impersonation of the self, a sort of country gaze. Larry Levis once compared Karl Marx to Jesus Christ when he said, "You can tell by the last letter of his name." He meant the X, and Levis cleverly tilted the T to a slanted cross. I have never met my grandfather, but the story goes that he approached enemy lines somewhere in Iran. When the guards in green uniforms saw his last name, Der Hovanessian, which means priest, they rejected his appellation—they said the country was infested with healers. So my grandfather, with quick wit, came up with the name "Kayzakian" which is pronounced Kai-tsok yown. The guards let him pass. In Armenian, Kai-tsok means lightning. So I guess you can say we arrived with a counterfeit name stolen from an electrical charge. My name has a lightning bolt transfixed into the way it flees the earth. I know we share a similar past. My Armenian-ness grounded in Iranian roots, rigged with backgammon and illegal poker. I double my wager that part of my ancestry belongs to a pack of immigrants aiming for a straight flush, when they all know—deep down—they have taken a bended road. These days, I've got a dent in my smile. It is hidden on the face I show the world, a very solitary, cryptic gesture. I wonder if my government name smiles at me when I look in the mirror. I wonder if that smile crosses borders looking for ways to name things just to survive. In a movie version, my smile is a 30-year-old street magician entertaining a European audience with his vanishing deck of cards on a random sidewalk. But for Americans, my smile would be killed off with sensational gore by an undercover cop for scratching my name on someone else's social security certificate; we'd be remembered as bribery money clipped inside a post card, greeting homeowners. I am afraid we are what makes the half-open window restless. What a strange time for a stranger. I just found out the virus has a patent, its name attached to serial numbers. When I was twenty-one, the judge called my name from a manila folder. He did not look up when he called me to the wooden stand. He used the case number attached to my file instead of the birth name I was given by my parents. I guess when a name is converted to numbers it means we are bad. I send you my love my friend, and my name scribed with its badness to the world.

Alexandra Umlas

Ode to Blue Nail Polish (at Home)

The shock of you makes me
five again—the soothing
wash of you, cotton candy,

blueberry, cerulean, serious navy,
your glint as I wash a dish, the play
of your flash on the keyboard,

the radiance of you, the expensive
coated-pot of you, your deep
magnified, as if each finger

were dipped in a sea, which stuck,
brilliant residue of fish scales, nails
turned marble, glossy gas flamed,

dart frog, dragonfly wing, suddenly
I am sixteen, driving down PCH,
ocean on every side, dawn brushed

from cuticle to lunula, to tip, covering
the parts of me that will be snipped
away. Your immortal singing—

Brian Harman

Found Fear in Evolution (2020 Edition)

Fucking
pandemic gone
viral, downward spiral,
rhymed lines, murder, murdering,
murder hornets, cicada killer wasps, wisps

of hope,
Pope, dope,
insertion of insensitive
jokes, Ron Jeremy is fucked
hardcore, bushfires, wildfires, pants on fire,

twin
hurricanes,
Sharknado 7 rumors,
kids in cages, Platypus milk,
Hydroxychloroquine snake oil, Weinstein,

wishful
guillotine,
unmasked, unmarked,
unemployed, uninformed uniformity,
un-United States, unitard, unicorn extinction,

Bible
locusts, poolside
feet licking bears, cancel
culture, woke, broke, fakeness,
rapeness, Karen crops, Ancient Aliens hair,

Brian Harman

high
school pep rally
PornHub theme drum solo,
guns, toting, loading, stroking,
Abbey Road deer reenactment, Pantoum

Master
Class, Taco Bell
Mexican Pizza removal,
hump, pump, stump, rump, dump,
Idiocracy/WALL-E future, climate change,

human
rights, suburban
goats, PE Chuck D,
BLM, SOS, RvW, RBG, lost
Mamba, lost Panther, cancer, no answer.

Stuck Pig

The pig, dead on the side of the road, didn't actually look to have bled all that much, but that saying kept chasing itself though Kourtney's head anyway. *Bleeding like a stuck pig.* In her head, the words were voiced with the impossibly-gruff rasp of some fictitious soldier, one who had seen death over and over but who still marveled at the especially catastrophic injuries.

Bleeding like a stuck pig.

Kourtney leaned over the hog (she'd decided that it was too big to be called a pig) and ignored her fiance, Chance, as he came scuffing up behind her on the gravel shoulder. He'd had to park the car and lock it. She'd hopped out of their little Subaru the second it had slowed enough and had almost tumbled headlong in her rush to investigate the massive hulk laying on its side in such an unlikely place.

The hog had just one tiny hole in it, maybe the size of a sharpie marker. A sole rivulet of blood ran from the minuscule wound. Its hair seemed thicker than a hog's hair should be, she could tell without touching it that it would be wiry, but strangely soft. Unbidden, she remembered that her dad had once had a boar's hair toothbrush.

"Holy shit," said Chance, "somebody fucking shot this guy!"

The hog's legs were locked straight, like some piece of furniture. It looked so utterly uncomfortable and stiff and not at all like a sleeping animal. Her hands were shaking fists even though she couldn't remember balling them up.

Chance had his phone out, he was walking toward the animal's head, like a hunter circling some great, downed mammoth.

"Someone just shot him and left him on the side of the road," he said, and his voice was coiled tight, braided with excitement and a little fear. She was glad he wouldn't have any reception this far out in the boonies, otherwise, he might be live streaming, beaming out a thousand thousand tiny clones of the stricken, paralytic animal, making the moment and all the suffering of it into something disposable. It would be wrong, and it made her wonder, for the briefest moment, if she really wanted to marry this man. She brushed the thought aside, not letting it form, then leaned in further.

The boar's black eye was gummy with road dust, but Kourtney could still see herself in it, could actually see the pure white clouds above her head. She almost touched his snout, bringing her hand so close that she expected to feel hot breath and felt a quick twist of sorrow at its absence. and then she didn't. She just let her hand hover there. The grass stretched out forever to either side of the road. They hadn't seen a car or farm or anything in hours.

She watched the body disappear into the rearview mirror and tried to decide what had kept her hand from reaching across that last millimeter of space, if closing that gap really even mattered at all. She imagined the hidden wound that had killed it, the farmer who'd fired the bullet, the last mad dash the hog must have made when it realized how little time it had left. It all seemed so remote, like another anonymous water tower or copse of trees disappearing into the horizon.

Something, then nothing, a droplet of rain disappearing back into the sea.

Arminé Iknadossian

Ocean Answers Back

After everything I did for you:
schools of fish, weightlessness,
all for you who swam out of ether,
crawled on four, walked on two.

You hungry lot wait at my feet,
so quick to cast sharp instruments into me.
I bore all of you, incubator and womb.
So much salt spilled for you.

Taste me brined and barnacled,
sifted through petroleum and tar.
I stick to your heels, my harpoon progeny,
give you ghosts of hidden cities,

graveyards of lost haircombs. I carry all of you
when you return whole or ash-ed.
Moon and I know all about mothers
who go mad over the ones they've made,

who drown their own babies in bathtubs.
My nightmares glow in the dark,
crowd together in the Marianna Trench.
My killer whales mourn stillbirths,

carry small carcasses aloft for weeks.
Even my icebergs weep. Here I am
with plastic heart and tinfoil ears,
hypodermic fingers and soda-bottles for shoes.

Arminé Iknadossian

I still have the old tires you sent me,
the rusted hood ornaments from fast cars you prize.
You wanted something more than calcium, urchin and krill.
Some manifest urge charged you towards land.

I still have soft waves for you and silver grunions,
sea-turtle hatchlings still blind their way towards me.
Look how they run to me with open arms empty of malice.
Isn't that what every mother wants?

Natalie Graham

Dark Lane Demo (Reprise)
after Drake

maybe I'll love you
one day   one day   one day
maybe
              later
coldcoldcold

listen, we a chorus, moody strings,
epic oohs and ahhs,

turning this, *she wanna fuck*,
into a concert of wolves

look at this open hand in my pocket

listentrust me, love   maybe

slaps on slaps on slaps
you know what it is

beating the block   wet
with bass

we out here hear   chea
you ride?
          you aint even outside

Natalie Graham

I'ma show you how
to stay ready, left—
listen, devils lurking in desires, love

real damn Devils
crouched in the brush
eyes flashlights, eyes white lilies
peeped open and shimmering

this a game, you young, right—
I'll call you, baby

love, drink up, I'ma show you
so many ways to feel
the dark

Joan Jobe Smith

I Can't Breathe

I can't breathe.
The smoke from the pyre burning me alive
because my name is Joan in Rouen chokes me.
Othello smothers me with a pillow.
Bill Sykes bludgeons me with his walking
stick till I fall to the floor, face down in Dickens dust.
Jack the Ripper slices as he writes his initials across my
throat.
A Nazi shaves my head and hands me a bar
of soap for my shower in Auschwitz

and right now I am watching a video
of a big cop sitting on my chest
as he laughs, tells me a joke, while
he punches me in the face with his big fists
a cop big enough to sign with the NFL
play first string, win a Super Bowl.

Have you ever had a big dude
with a big ass like that
sit on your chest?
Scream hyena in your
face?
Knee on your neck.
I have.

Joan Jobe Smith

Cracks your rib bones,
busts your eardrums
and carotid
and breaks your heart.

That happened to me nearly 50 years ago
and it just happened to me again right now as
I watch it on a video here in my dining room
of him, you, me,
in the privacy of my own home,
minding my own business
now minding his, each our own business
and I can't
BREATHE.

Can YOU?

Brendan Constantine

The Naming of Boats

I'm the only one still awake. The rooms
mumble, dreaming. Through the window
the street shines like a fish. When

did the rain stop. Why can't I hear
the clock. Perhaps it's sleeping, too.
Why is a house more full of the past

before dawn and not after. Once,
when I was a scream, a woman peered
into my crib, her face enormous,

saying things. She reached down
and set a boat on my pillow, one made
of paper and wire. Then she hushed

and fled, though she stayed close
to mind. I think I ate the boat.
When things are quiet like this,

so quiet you could hear smoke,
I feel it drift, little red soaked skiff,
pilotless. You're supposed to name

ships after women, but I don't know
who she was. I can't even name
this year, this hour, this house sunk
to the bottom of the night.

Kevin Ridgeway

The Emperor's New Virus

He never robbed me of my time
or space in my head because
I knew he was a trigger
for the mental illness I've been
diagnosed with for years
that some still think is an act
of welfare fraud. He was
elected four years ago on
my 34th birthday, a day
after Leonard Cohen died
and a few days before
Leon Russell's voice
went silent after it sang
of being a stranger
in a strange land. They
handcuffed me for going off
my medication while
angry about an election
of a television sideshow
of people who do not
give a fuck about people
like me as it awakened
the demons hidden inside.
His transition into
the White House was
covered in real time
on the news channels

Kevin Ridgeway

that flashed on the television
across from my cell
in County Jail, terrified
of the world I wanted
to be released into.
I did the time and I paid
for my crime, but here
we are again, my response
weighed down by years
of righteous indignation
inside of my dead mother's
foolish heart. I turn the
television on mute
and wonder what a crime
against humanity it would be
if he had to march naked out
of the White House and into
the arms of Gary Busey
and Meat Loaf, the only
two people who will talk
to him after they got him
cast on Celebrity Rehab, and
it will be a gala day when
I can dance on his grave
with a strand of piss
to put out the eternal flame
of his exposed tyranny.

Zubin Shourie

2020

It's a snowball rolling down a hill;
with every second it gradually grows in size
and picks up speed.

It's casually cruising down the road
and out of nowhere getting T-boned. No matter how much
you try to avoid this moment

there is nothing you can do to stop it.
It's the struggle of fighting off weeds in a garden;
no matter how many times you go out and pluck them,
they come back to torture you.

Will this year ever come to an end,
or will this mask forever hide my smile?

T. Anders Carson

Letter from the front

To Canada Post Management, Canada Post Workers and Customers:

It is a sunny Sunday evening and the sunset is going to be fantastic. It was so chilly today that we actually put on a fire to get the dampness out of the house. I worked out in the forest and was greeted by many mosquitoes but rejoiced when I saw the dragonflies muscle in. This week the parcels were there and they will be there for awhile yet. I know the morning will be busy but that's a Monday working at Canada Post. We will do it and get as much out as we can and then carry on with our duties.

I read once in a Chekhov short story and he said this will pass. In times of sadness it is helpful. This will pass. In times of stress. This will pass. In times of great joy. This will pass. A real zinger that has stuck.

I did it again. I turned on the TV and saw angry protesters, angry police in riot gear, the night sky filling with fire. You know you shouldn't. It's like when you're a small child and you find some matches. You light one and get a whee rush. Well it's the same with watching the news these days. You find the station, fixate on it for a little spell and then you get a rush. It's so turbulent. The way it's covered by masked people, in front of masked people, being lorded over by masked people. I did get a glimmer of hope. It was from the sheriff of Flint, MI. Flint has fallen on hard times. The auto industry moved out leaving people without jobs. The local water supply was tainted, leaving people to drink unsafe water. And this past week the sheriff got up in front of the protesters in the town. And what did he do? He took off his helmet and shield and put down his baton and asked them 'What do you want me to do?' They chanted *walk with us, walk with us, walk with us.* And he did...

I got in touch with a friend from years ago this week. His mother had passed. He was the first Canadian publisher to choose my work. We've brought our kids to pow wows together. I've gone to an NHL game with him and many launch parties for our books. It was so good to get caught up. I don't know if I would have had this chance unless there was COVID. It makes you realize how important friendship, closeness (not distance) and the memories of going through things together. That is what we will all take out of this. It does affect us on some plane. It affects us in our sleeping patterns (hands up how many have had strange dreams!) how it's challenging to put on a brave face. I think back to how my grandmother did it during the war. Five years her husband gone to fight overseas. He was one of the lucky ones to come back. But like many he was a shell of a man who didn't speak of what he had seen or done. They did it and survived. We will too.

I guess this is turning into a pandemic fatigue instalment. It happens. I'm acknowledging it but am thankful that on Friday night when we got a paycheck I could go and line up to get food. I remember as a child visiting Russia and seeing the line ups for food. It was in 1982. Not many people got to go behind the Iron Curtain but there I was with my family on a trip. Not a Griswold trip to Wally World but one to see how the other side lived. I'm glad my parents took the chance to take us there. I remember weeping tears thinking that they would whisk us away to some Siberian camp. But that's what imagination is and a child's perception. Now I'm an adult. I look after the safety of those in our office. Check in to see if everyone is doing OK. And know that sometimes it's alright to let the silence reign.

Today is a new dawn. The birds are vividly chirping. The dew is wet, wet, wet on the grass and we will get through these times together. By talking, sharing and caring. One package at a time. One needed cheque at a time. One birthday greeting at a time. Be safe out there.

Without prejudice and in solidarity,

Anders Carson

Lanark Post Master and Ontario Director of CPAA

A. León lives, writes and votes in Southern California. She has spent the better part of the quarantine trying not to compose work solely about disease, moral bankruptcy and isolation. She has a fool-proof coconut macaroon recipe. She remains hopeful about the future.

Alexandra Umlas is the author of the full-length poetry collection *At the Table of the Unknown* (Moon Tide Press, 2019). She holds an M.F.A. in Poetry from California State University, Long Beach, and an M.Ed. in Cross-cultural Education.

At the age of three, **Arminé Iknadossian** was called a "shitty Armenian" while playing outside in Beirut, Lebanon. A soldier shoved her, but she did not fall down. Instead, she and her family moved to California. Author of *All That Wasted Fruit* (Main Street Rag), learn more at armineiknadossian.com.

Arthur Kayzakian is a poet and editor. He was born in Tehran, Iran. His family sought political asylum in London when he was three years old to escape the Iranian Revolution. He is a contributing editor at *Poetry International*. His chapbook, *My Burning City,* was a finalist for the Locked Horn Press Chapbook Prize and Two Sylvias Press Chapbook Prize. He is a recipient of the Minas Savvas Fellowship, and his poems and translations have appeared in or are forthcoming from several publications including *Taos Journal of International Poetry & Art,* *COUNTERCLOCK, Chicago Review, Locked Horn Press* and *Prairie Schooner.*

Aruni Wijesinghe is a project manager, ESL teacher, erstwhile belly dance instructor and occasional sous chef. She has been published in anthologies and journals both nationally and internationally and has collections forthcoming with Moon Tide Press and Silver Star Laboratory. She lives a quiet life with Jeff, Jack and Josie.

Ben Trigg is the co-host of Two Idiots Peddling Poetry at the Ugly Mug in Orange, California. His full length collection *Kindness from a Dark God* came out on Moon Tide Press in 2007. He co-edited the anthology *Don't Blame the Ugly Mug: 10 Years of 2 Idiots Peddling Poetry* published by Tebot Bach. When all else fails, Ben goes to Disneyland.

Brendan Constantine is a nationally recognized poet based in Los Angeles. His work has appeared in many of the nation's standards, including *Poetry, Best American Poetry, Prairie Schooner, Poetry Daily, Tin House, Ploughshares, Field, Virginia Quarterly,* and *Poem-a-Day*. His most recent collections are *Dementia, My Darling* (2016) from Red Hen Press and *Bouncy Bounce* (2018), a chapbook from Blue Horse Press.

Brian Harman was raised in Orange County, California, where he can be found trying craft beers and being a proud dad. His work has been published in *Chiron Review, Nerve Cowboy, Misfit Magazine,* etc. His first collection, *Suddenly, All Hell Broke Loose!!!* was published by Picture Show Press in 2020.

Burt Shultz , a rogue and world traveler in a time before our time.

Cynthia Alessandra Briano is director of the *Rapp Saloon Reading Series*. She is also founder of Love On Demand Global, an organization which creates custom-ordered poetry for charity. She is a graduate student at University of California Riverside Palm Desert MFA program.

A 2019 PEN America Emerging Voices Fellow, **Dare Williams** is a Queer HIV-positive poet, artist, rooted in Southern California. He has received fellowships from John Ashbury Home School and The Frost Place. Dare's poetry has been nominated for a Pushcart Prize and he is a two-time finalist for *Blood Orange Review's* contest. His work has been featured in *Cultural Weekly, Bending Genres, THRUSH* and *Exposition Review*. He is currently working on his first poetry collection.

Donna Hilbert's latest book is *Gravity: New & Selected Poems*, (Tebot Bach, 2018). She is a monthly contributing writer to the on-line journal *Verse-Virtual*. She is eager to resume leading in-person workshops and hugging her friends. Learn more at www.donnahilbert.com

Dr. **Donny Jackson** is a lifelong poet, clinical psychologist, and Emmy Award-winning documentary television producer. His debut volume of poetry is *boy* (Silver Star Laboratory, 2020).

Elisabeth Dahl lives and works in Baltimore, Maryland. Her short pieces have been published by *American Short Fiction, NPR.org, The Rumpus, Necessary Fiction*, and other outlets and journals. She's also the author-illustrator of the middle-grade novel *Genie Wishes* (Abrams). Her website is elisabethdahl.com.

Fred Voss has been a machinist and written about it for over 40 years. Eight reading tours of England and 3 Bloodaxe Books poetry collections later, he's still carving metal and poems. His latest full-length collection, *Hammers and Hearts of the Gods*, was selected a 2009 Book of the Year by the Morning Star (London).

George Hammons is a southern California poet and photographer whose poems are often about social justice, family and love. George's poems are usually straightforward and to the point, yet they are capable of projecting images that are deeply personal, yet familiar and accessible.
George's poetry has been published in *Pacific Review, Cadence Collective,* and *American Mustard*. He is author of two chapbooks *Hungry to Bed – Love Poems* (Arroyo Seco press, 2018), and *Witness* (Picture Show Press, 2020).

James Evert Jones has curated and hosted spoken word events for over 30 years, from Tarzana to Redondo Beach. James' work has been featured in *Voices from Leimert Park Redux* and *Onyx: Spoken Word* among others.
James is a recipient of the 2019 President's Volunteer Service Award.

Joan Jobe Smith, founding editor of PEARL (1974-2017) and Bukowski Review, received her BA from CSULB and MFA from UCI; her work's appeared internationally in more than 1000 journals. Her recent poetry collection from NYQ *Moonglow Á Go-Go*, is available on Amazon.

John Brantingham was Sequoia and Kings Canyon National Parks' first poet laureate. His work has been featured in hundreds of magazines, *Writers Almanac* and *The Best Small Fictions 2016*. His books include *Crossing the High Sierra* (Cholla Needles Press) and *Life, Orange to Pear* (Bamboo Dart Press). He teaches at Mt. San Antonio College.

Juan Delgado is Professor Emeritus in the English Department at California State University, San Bernardino, he chaired the English and Communication Studies Departments and served as the university's interim provost. His collections of poetry include *Green Web* (1994), published by the University of Georgia Press and selected by poet Dara Weir for the Contemporary Poetry Prize; *El Campo* (1998), a collaboration with the Chicano painter Simon Silva and published by Capra Press; and *Rush of Hands* (2003), published by the University of Arizona Press. His most recent book, *Vital Signs* (2013), was a collaboration with photographer Thomas McGovern and won the Before Columbus Foundation's American Book Award.

Julia Ingalls is primarily an essayist. Her work has appeared in *The Los Angeles Times*, *Salon*, *The Nervous Breakdown*, and *The Los Angeles Review of Books*, among other publications.

K. Andrew Turner writes queer, literary, and speculative prose and poetry. In 2013, he founded East Jasmine Review—an electronic literary journal. His full-length poetry collection *Heart, Mind, Blood, Skin* is now available from Finishing Line Press. He was a semifinalist for the 2016 Luminaire Award. You can find more at his website: www.kandrewturner.com

Kareem Tayyar's novel, *The Prince of Orange County* (Pelekinesis), received the 2020 Eric Hoffer Award for Young Adult Fiction.

Kevin Ridgeway is the author of *Too Young to Know* (Stubborn Mule Press) and nine chapbooks of poetry including *Grandma Goes to Rehab* (Analog Submission Press, UK). His most recent work can be found in *Slipstream, Chiron Review, Nerve Cowboy, Plainsongs, San Pedro River Review, The Cape Rock, Trailer Park Quarterly, Main Street Rag, Cultural Weekly* and *The American Journal of Poetry*, among others. He lives and writes in Long Beach, CA.

Lisbeth Coiman Is a bilingual writer from Venezuela. Her work has appeared in *La Bloga, Entropy, Acentos, Lady/Liberty/Lit, Nailed, Hip Mama, Rabid Oaks, Cultural Weekly, Resonancias, The Altadena Literary Review,* and *Accolades: A Women Who Submit Anthology*. Her memoir, *I Asked the Blue Heron* (2017) explores the intersection between immigration and mental health.

Natalie J. Graham, a native of Gainesville, Florida, earned her M.F.A. in Creative Writing at the University of Florida. Her first poetry collection, *Begin with a Failed Body* (University of Georgia Press, 2017), was selected by Kwame Dawes for the 2016 Cave Canem Poetry Prize.

Ra Avis is an award-winning blogger, and the author of *Sack Nasty: Prison Poetry* (2016), *Dinosaur-Hearted* (2018), and *Flowers and Stars* (2018).
She is a once-upon-a-time inmate, a reluctantly-optimistic widow, and a generational storyteller. Ra reads her poetry live at events throughout Southern California, and writes regularly at Rarasaur.com.

Scott Noon Creley holds an MFA in poetry from CSU Long Beach, and a BA in writing from UC Riverside. He is the founding chairman of San Gabriel Valley Literary Festival, a non-profit literacy foundation heading into its seventh year. His first collection of poetry, *Digging a Hole to the Moon*, is available from Spout Hill Press.

Shana Nicholson-Morgan holds a degree in English from the University of Louisiana. She has published work with *Superficial Flesh, Red Booth Review, Birmingham Arts Journal* and several others. She lives in Birmingham, Alabama with her wife and daughter.

Stephanie Barbé Hammer is a 6 time Pushcart Prize nominee with work in the *Bellevue Literary Review, Pearl, Hayden's Ferry, Isthmus,* and the *Gold Man Review*. Stephanie was born in Manhattan and now wanders the woods of rural Washington State looking for a taco truck, a dry cleaner and someone to talk to.

Steve Ramirez hosts the weekly reading series, Two Idiots Peddling Poetry. A former member of the Laguna Beach Slam Team, he's also a former organizer of the Orange County Poetry Festival and former member of the Five Penny Poets in Huntington Beach.

Suhasini Yeeda's work has been published or is forthcoming with *Packingtown Review, LARB, The Indian Review, Madcap Review,* and *Ms. Magazine*. She is a two-time Pushcart Prize nominee and a nominee for Best American Short Stories and Best of the Net. Suhasini is from Dallas, lives in Los Angeles, and has an MFA from Sarah Lawrence College.

T. Anders Carson has had his poems published in 37 countries including translations into French, Greek, Japanese and Swedish. He has written 5 books of poetry. His latest is titled *Unfortunately, Thanks for Everything* from Pelekinesis Press. He is a Helene Wurlitzer Foundation Fellow, and a member of the League of Canadian Poets. He has read his work from Los Angeles to London including stops in Cairo, Paris, Stockholm and Swansea. He currently resides on the outskirts of Portland in Ontario, and lives with his wife and cat.

Terri Niccum's most recent chapbook is *Dead Letter Box* from Moon Tide Press. Her poems have also featured in *Golden Street Car Literary Journal* and in *Making Up,* an anthology from Picture Book Press. She gets knocked down but she gets up again, leaning on poetry.

Zubin Shourie lives in Los Angeles. He is in the 11th grade and currently studies Creative Writing with Brendan Constantine at the Windward School.

www.ingramcontent.com/pod-product-compliance
Lightning Source LLC
Chambersburg PA
CBHW070942250626
47159CB00009B/3347